D1108028

NILA'S PERFECT COAT

BY

NORENE PAULSON

ILLUSTRATED BY

MARIA MOLA

beaming books

MINNEAPOLIS

To Andrea: Thank you for once again believing in me and my words.—*NP*

For my mom, who taught me to never compare myself to the ones that had it better than me but to the ones that had it worse and needed my help.—*MM*

Text copyright © 2023 Norene Paulson
Illustrations by Maria Mola, copyright © 2023 Beaming Books

28 27 26 25 24 23 22   1 2 3 4 5 6 7 8

Hardcover ISBN: 978-1-5064-8581-2
eBook ISBN: 978-1-5064-8582-9

Library of Congress Cataloging-in-Publication Data

Names: Paulson, Norene, author. | Mola, Maria, illustrator.
Title: Nila's perfect coat / by Norene Paulson ; illustrated by Maria Mola.
Description: Minneapolis, MN : Beaming Books, 2023. | Audience: Ages 3-8. |
  Summary: When Nila finds the perfect coat at the thrift store, her mom
  says no because her one from last year fits just fine, so she sets out
  to buy it herself, but realizes maybe it is the perfect coat for someone
  else.
Identifiers: LCCN 2022013610 (print) | LCCN 2022013611 (ebook) | ISBN
  9781506485812 (hardcover) | ISBN 9781506485829 (ebook)
Subjects: CYAC: Coats--Fiction. | Kindness--Fiction. | Generosity--Fiction.
  | LCGFT: Picture books.
Classification: LCC PZ7.1.P38535 Ni 2023 (print) | LCC PZ7.1.P38535
  (ebook) | DDC [E]--dc23
LC record available at https://lccn.loc.gov/2022013610
LC ebook record available at https://lccn.loc.gov/2022013611

VN0004589; 9781506485812; DEC2022

Beaming Books
PO Box 1209
Minneapolis, MN 55440-1209
Beamingbooks.com

Nila loved treasure hunting.

Whenever she outgrew her shirts or jeans or coats,
she and her mom headed to the thrift store.

"You never know what treasures you'll find if you dig long enough,"
Mom always said.

And dig they did:
through shelves of books, board games, and puzzles,
bins of stuffed animals,
and racks of color-tagged clothes.
Some gently worn. Others like new.

SWEATERS

PANTS

LONG SLEEVE
SHIRTS

KIDS
COATS

8$

"It's so warm," said Nila. "And fits perfectly."

"You don't need another coat," said Mom. "Last year's fits you fine for now." Nila's heart sank.

Last year's coat. The coat with the tricky zipper and the well-worn trim.

"Please, Momma? I still have some of the money Daddy
gave me for my birthday."

Mom sighed. "Put the coat back, Nila. I'll let you and your
dad decide together."

On the way home, all Nila could think about was the puffy, brightly colored coat with its easy-glide zipper.

In the morning, Nila rushed out the door before Mom could remind her to take her coat.

On the bus, Nila was the only one NOT wearing a coat—until Lily's stop.

When Lily glanced her way, Nila smiled, but Lily looked away.

Without coats, Nila and Lily had to stay inside
for recess.

Nila asked Lily if she wanted to play a game,
but Lily wanted to color . . . by herself.

When the bell rang at the end of the day, Mr. Hawthorne said, "Remember your coats on Monday, girls, if you want to go out for recess." Nila gave a thumbs-up. Lily kept her head down and shuffled out the door.

On Saturday when Dad picked Nila up for the weekend, she had her birthday money tucked in the pocket of her old coat.

"Can we stop at the thrift store?" she asked. "I want to buy something with my birthday money, but Mom said to ask you first."

Hopefully, the coat was still there.

It was!

"Do you really need two coats?" asked Dad.

"No . . . but I really want this one," she said as she twirled around in front of the mirror.

Dad looked at her and smiled. "You decide."

At the checkout, Nila handed the cashier
eight dollars and skipped out the door
with the thrift store coat stuffed in a large
shopping bag.

On the drive home on Sunday, Nila noticed a For Sale sign in Lily's front yard.

"Lily's moving?" she asked.

"Her family's going through a hard time," said Dad.

Nila wasn't sure what Dad meant, but now all she could think about was Lily in her too-big sweatshirt coloring by herself.

By the time she got home . . .

Her new coat didn't shine quite so brightly.

At least not hanging next to her old coat,
which Nila knew DID still fit her just fine.

At dinner Nila pushed her pasta around her plate. She didn't feel like eating. Finally she said, "I don't think Lily has a winter coat."

"You don't?" Mom asked.

"No." And then Nila told Mom all about Lily's too-big sweatshirt and how sad Lily seemed.

"And now I have two coats,
so I was thinking . . ."

Mom gave Nila a quick hug. "I like what you're thinking. I'll call Lily's mom and see what she says."

"Let's go!"

FOR SALE

And when the recess bell rang on Monday,

EVERYONE went outside.

SHARE THE WARMTH: KIDS HELPING KIDS

Every year when the temperature drops, thousands of kids living in colder climates don't have winter coats to keep them warm.

HOW YOU CAN HELP

Here are three ways you can be like Nila and share the warmth of a winter coat through national nonprofit One Warm Coat:

DONATE COATS

- Ask family members and friends for coats they've outgrown or no longer wear.
- Check to make sure zippers work and there are no missing buttons or snaps and no holes or stains.
- Ask an adult to visit One Warm Coat's website (www.onewarmcoat.org) to find a coat donation site near you.
- Bring coats to the nearest drop-off site during designated collection hours.

ORGANIZE A SCHOOL FUNDRAISER

- Ask your school administrator for permission to organize a One Warm Coat Challenge. The grade or classroom raising the most money could receive a reward like a pizza party or an extra recess.
- Determine when the challenge begins and how long it will run.
- Create signs and posters to promote the challenge and to raise awareness of the need for warm coats. Post in the cafeteria, hallways, and other common areas.
- Decorate donation containers.
- With adult help, collect and count the money for each grade or class at the end of each day. Ramp up the competition by posting each class or grade's daily totals.
- On the final day of the challenge, add up the totals. Announce the challenge winner.
- With the money raised, buy gently used coats at local thrift stores and give to an area coat drive, OR donate the money directly to One Warm Coat.

HOLD A "SHARE THE WARMTH" COAT DRIVE

- A coat drive is a great community service project. Ask for adult help to visit One Warm Coat's website (www.onewarmcoat.org) to learn about their six-step coat drive program.

- Determine a drop-off location. Consider community locations like libraries, community centers, schools, or faith organizations. Ask permission.

- Decide when to hold the coat drive and set drop-off times. Always have at least two people, including an adult, at the drop-off site during drop-off hours.

- Decorate donation containers. Use clean large boxes, plastic tubs, or trash cans.

- Tell your family, friends, and neighbors. Ask adults to promote the coat drive through local news outlets and on social media. (They can find resources on www.onewarmcoat.org.)

- Create signs to post on community bulletin boards. To make it easy to find, post large poster-board signs near the drop-off site.

- Sort through donated coats. Be sure zippers work and there are no missing buttons or snaps. Look for holes or stains. Ask yourself, Would I wear this coat?

- Set aside any unacceptable coats for recycling at the nearest textile recycling location.

- To donate coats, find a donation site near you on One Warm Coat's website (www.onewarmcoat.org).

- Drop coats off at the nearest site.

- For more how-to ideas, visit One Warm Coat's website at www.onewarmcoat.org, click the "Hold a Coat Drive" tab, and register. When you do, you will receive a Welcome Packet and step-by-step instructions on how to organize your coat drive, plus free resources including a goal thermometer, flyers, and graphics. The site also includes a Coat Donation Locator Map link, making it easier to find donation sites near you.

Norene Paulson writes picture books that celebrate friendship, acceptance, and inclusion. She is the author of *Benny's True Colors* and *What's Silly Hair Day with No Hair?* A former language arts teacher, Norene is passionate about sharing her love of words with young readers. She's a member of SCBWI and lives in Iowa.

Maria Mola is an illustrator from Barcelona currently living in Boston with her husband and their three children. She has illustrated *Sparkle Boy, Maya Papaya, Koala Challah,* and more.